S0-ABC-204

About the Book

Anya was tired of working in the ant nest. All day and all night she carried the queen's eggs, looked after the new babies, and took loads of old cocoons to the trash pile. And, if that wasn't enough, bossy Matilda was always telling her what to do. Anya was fed up with the routine. She wanted a little adventure in her life.

Then one day a dark cloud hovered overhead and Anya got more adventure than she had bargained for. A tremendous torrent of rain drenched the nest, threatening to drown the entire colony.

Anya bravely led the rescue operation until she found herself separated from her companions and plunging down a turbulent stream away from the nest.

Penny Pollock has created an original and endearing character in Anya, a small black ant. She offers a fascinating glimpse of ant life along with a dramatic and funny story.

Ants Don't Get Sunday Off

by Penny Pollock

illustrated by
Lorinda Bryan Cauley

G.P. PUTNAM'S SONS • NEW YORK

For my parents, Bill and Eleanor Morrow,
who showed me the wonder of life.

Text copyright © 1978 by Penny Pollock
Illustrations copyright © 1978 by Lorinda Bryan Cauley
All rights reserved. Published simultaneously in
Canada by Longman Canada Limited, Toronto.
Printed in the United States of America
06209

Library of Congress Cataloging in Publication Data
Pollock, Penny. Ants don't get Sunday off.
Summary: Anya, a hard-working ant, longs for
adventure but gets more than she bargained for
when a heavy rainstorm disturbs the ant nest.
[1. Ants—Fiction] I. Cauley, Lorinda Bryan.
II. Title.
PZ7.P765An [Fic] 78-8283
ISBN 0-399-61129-0 lib. bdg.

Contents

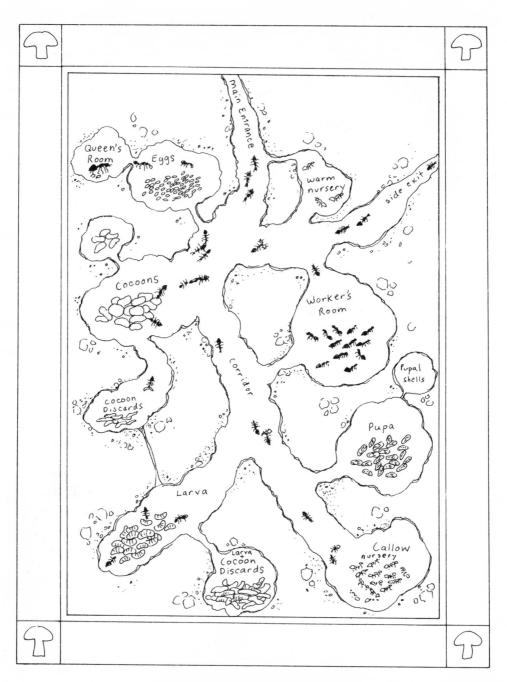

Queen's Room

Eggs

Main Entrance

warm nursery

side exit

Cocoons

Worker's Room

Pupal shells

Corridor

Cocoon Discards

Pupa

Larva

Larva + Cocoon Discards

Callow nursery

Map of Anya's Nest

1/Life Under Ground

Anya sat down to rest

in the underground hallway.

She was a small black ant.

All of her life

she had lived in the nest

under the flat gray rock.

Every day she worked and worked and worked.

Every night she worked and worked and worked.

Matilda, the Head Worker Ant, came by
and saw Anya sitting down.
"The Queen needs workers
to carry her new eggs," she said crossly.
"I am resting a minute," Anya told her.
"There is no time to rest," Matilda said.

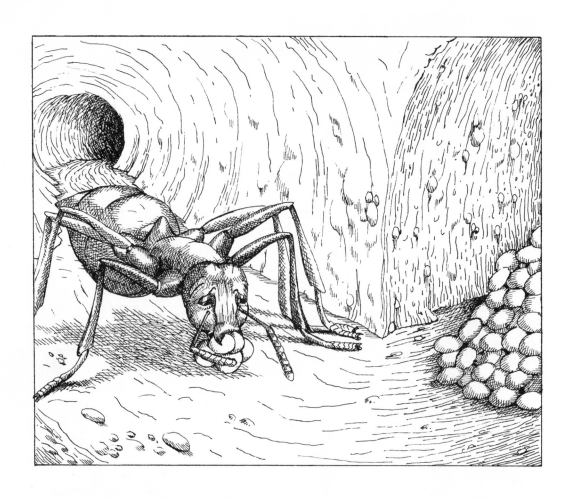

Anya went back to work.

But she was still tired.

"What I need is a small holiday," she said,

as she glued a mound of new eggs together

and carried them to the warm nursery.

"What I need is a short trip," she said,
as she pulled a baby ant from its cocoon
and licked it.
"What I need is a small adventure," she said,
as she stretched out the baby ant's legs.
Then she sat down to rest again.

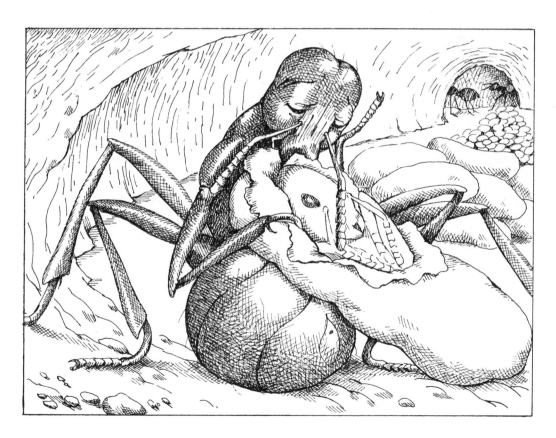

She combed her feelers with the comb
on her left front leg.
Then Matilda came by.
"There is no time for that," she said.
"These old cocoons must be carried
to the trash pile."

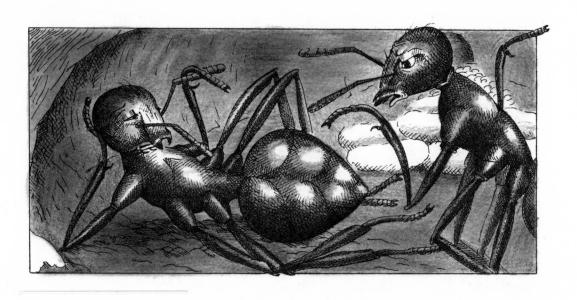

"I am tired of working," Anya said.
"Could I have Sunday off?"
Matilda just frowned.

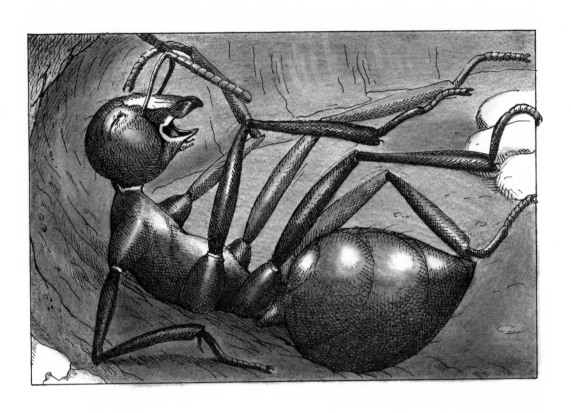

Anya yawned.

Then she washed her face.

When she was finished,

she knew that she did not want to sit.

And she did not want to work.

Suddenly she kicked up her six heels

all at once and called out, "I want to live!"

But she had forgotten that she was

in the cramped hallway under the gray rock.

She banged her left feeler

on the dirt ceiling and bent it to one side.

"Oh, rooshnik!" Anya said,

picking herself up and going back to work.

It seemed as if her life would never change.

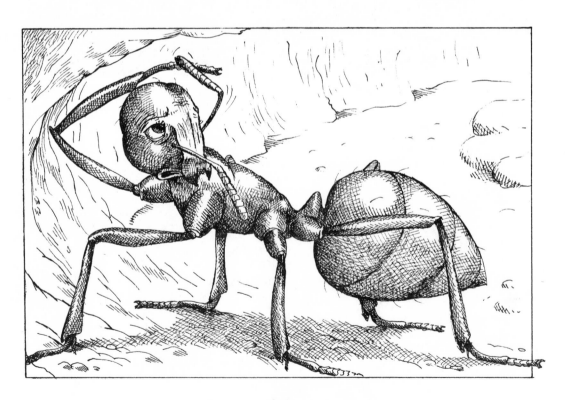

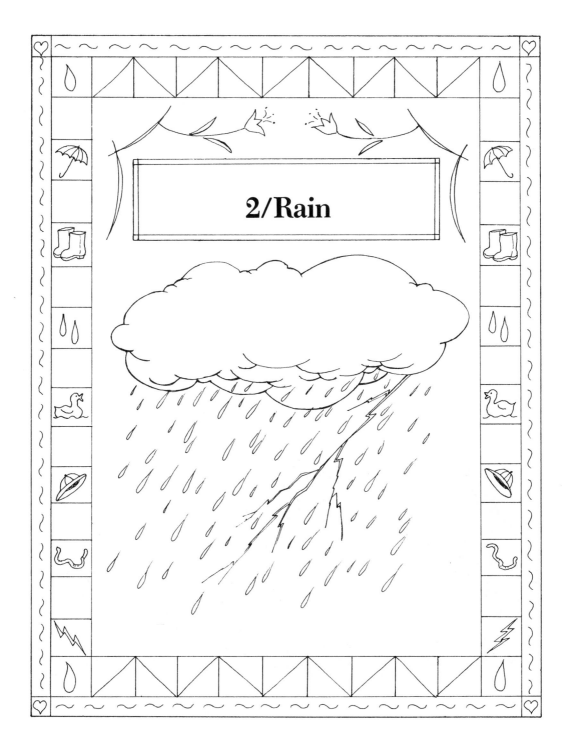

2/Rain

Then one morning a great black cloud
hung over the flat gray rock.
Anya did not see the cloud.
She was underground, working.
Rain fell from the great black cloud
onto the rock.
It pounded down for days and days
and nights and nights.
Finally the rain found
the front-door opening of the nest.

It rushed down the hallway.

Water filled every room,

even the warm nursery.

Anya ran for her life.

So did the other ants.

They tumbled on top of one another,

scrambling for the doorway.

Anya was almost at the doorway
when she remembered the Queen.
"Stop," Anya called loudly.
"We have to save the Queen."
The other ants tried to push past her,
but Anya would not budge.
She knew her duty
even if she did want a holiday.

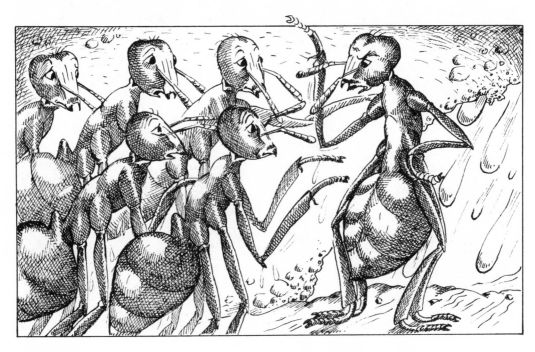

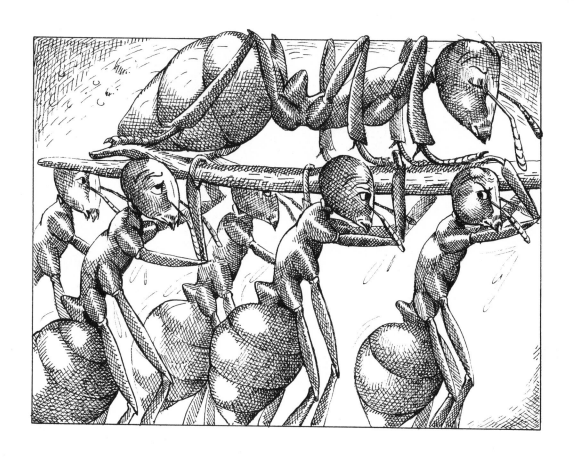

The other ants felt cross and wet and scared,

but they knew Anya was right.

Together they dragged the Queen

through the swampy hallway.

They carried her out to high ground

on top of a twig.

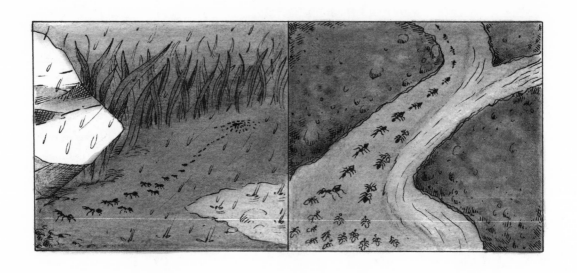

"And now for the baby ants," Anya said.

Some of the worker ants stayed

to lick the Queen dry.

The rest followed Anya back into the nest.

The hallway floor was muddy

and the ants slipped and slid and struggled.

Finally the baby ants were carried to safety.

Some of the workers stayed

to lick the baby ants dry.

Then Anya said, "We can't forget the eggs."

The rest of the ants

followed Anya once more into the nest,

because they could see she knew her duty.

Down the damp and dangerous hallway they went

to the nursery far under the ground.

Each worker picked up an egg and

struggled back up the hallway.

Anya led the way.

Finally the Queen, the baby ants,

and the eggs were above the ground.

The rest of the workers licked them dry,

but Anya was worried.

Some eggs were missing, she was sure.

Alone Anya crawled under the flat gray rock.

The mud stuck to her feet

but she sloshed slowly down,

down to the nursery.

There were three eggs left.

The water was nearly up to her middle.

Even Anya knew there could be

no more trips down the muddy hallway.

She would have to carry all three eggs.

Carefully Anya squeezed the eggs

tightly in her jaw and started for safety.

Twice she was almost stuck in the mud.

Once she was blocked by a boulder of sand.

She dug around it.

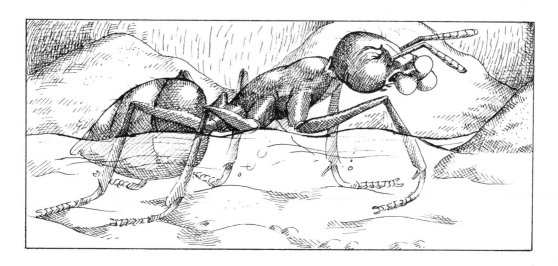

At last, tired all the way through,

she reached the safe outdoors.

But when she looked for the other ants,

she could not see a single one.

24

3/The Trip

There was no time to rest.

First she would take care of the eggs.

Then she would find the other ants.

The eggs would be safe on top of a mushroom.

She climbed up a mushroom stem,

but lost her balance.

She slipped down the wet stem

and fell in a puddle on her back.

She waved all six legs in the air

and yelled, *"Help!"*

That made her drop the eggs.

Worse still, water started to fill

her joints, and she could hardly breathe.

Half drowned, she watched as one by one

the eggs were carried away by the rainwater.

Anya got mad.

"I will get them no matter what," she said.

With all the strength she had left,

she twisted and turned

until she flipped onto her feet.

She splashed to the side of the puddle.

She crawled out, wet, tired, and determined.

After a giant shake to get the water

out of her joints,

Anya limped after the eggs.

There was no time to lick oil

into her joints, although they needed it.

Water was everywhere.

She searched for the eggs.

They were gone!

Then she looked for her nest,

but she could not find it, either.

Anya climbed up a long dandelion stem.

She stood on top of the yellow blossom

and searched for the flat gray rock.

All she saw was water.

"Oh, rooshnik!" she said,

to make herself feel better.

It did not help.

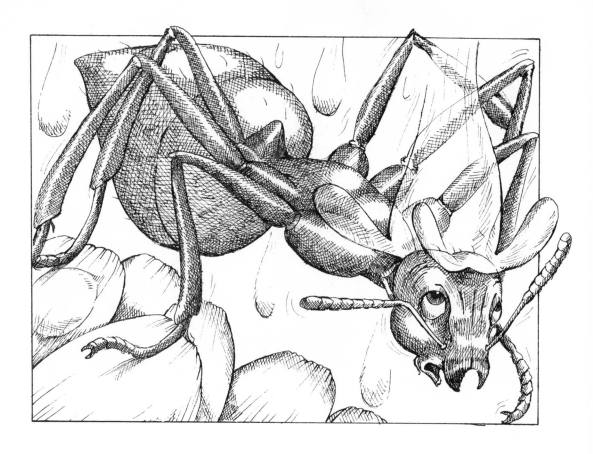

She was tired and wet and lonely.

She had lost three eggs and her nest.

She started to lick her front left leg

for comfort when a huge raindrop

hit her on the head.

It knocked her off the dandelion.

She landed on an upturned oak leaf

in a pool of water.

For a minute she lay still,

too scared to think.

Then the oak leaf began to turn circles

in the water.

Anya felt dizzy.

She crawled to the stem of the leaf
and held on.
She had just grabbed hold
when the leaf tumbled into a ditch.
The ditch water raced on
until it fell into a stream.
Anya was in for a wild trip.

It ended with a crash against a log.

The crash flung her through the air.

Luckily she landed on soft sand.

Anya stood up shakily and tried her legs.

All six still worked.

She tried her feelers.

They both still worked.

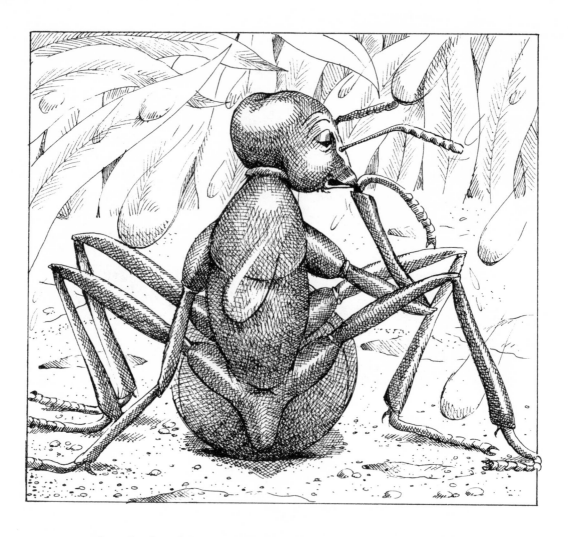

She licked herself dry and oiled her joints.

That always made her feel better.

"All I need is a short rest," she said.

"Then I must find my nest."

34

4/A Sweet Smell

After a short rest, Anya raised her feelers

to smell for her nest.

She did smell something.

Was it her nest?

No, but it was a sweet smell,

and Anya was very hungry.

She was as hungry as an ant

with two empty stomachs can be.

She waded through the grass forest

toward the sweet smell.

It was getting closer.

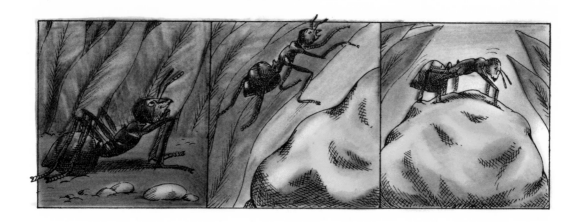

Then she saw what she had smelled.

It was huge and pink.

It sparkled with the wetness from the rain.

It smelled wonderful.

Anya was so excited that she did not notice

that the rain had stopped.

She hunched down and then sprang up.

She landed squarely on all six feet.

And every foot got stuck!

She had landed on a gigantic mountain

of chewed bubble gum!

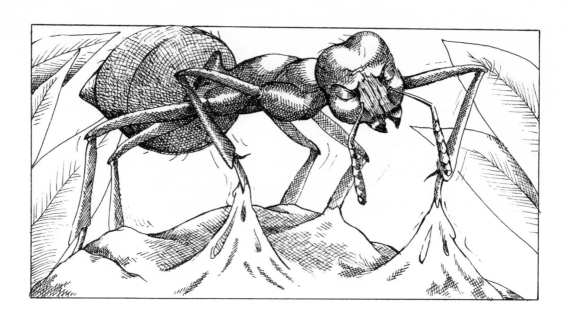

When she tried to pull one leg free,

the other five sunk in deeper.

She was in gum up to her knees.

Anya was in trouble and she knew it.

Every time she moved, she sunk in deeper.

All she could do was sit and rest and think.

She thought about her nest.

She missed all the other ants.

Even Matilda.

"Help!" Anya called.

No one answered.

She was stuck all night.

It was a long, dark, lonely night.

In the morning she said,

"I am going to get off here no matter what."

She waved her feelers in the air

to find someone to help her.

There was no one there.

She stopped with a jerk.

She had just smelled something wonderful.

Home!

It was only a small whiff,

but Anya knew it was her nest.

She had to get off the bubble gum.

There was only one way out.

She started right away.

She ate and ate and ate.

Her two stomachs bulged.

She ate more and more and more.

She felt sick. But still she ate more.

Two legs were free.

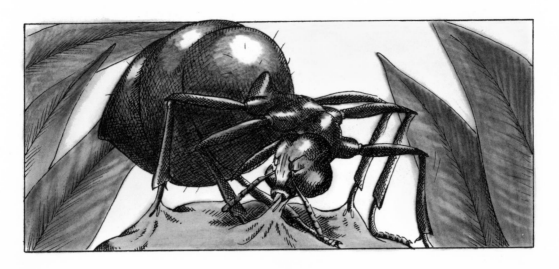

She ate and ate and ate.

She thought her stomachs would pop open.

Five legs were free.

But she could not eat another bite.

Not even one.

"Well, maybe a small one," she said.

But as soon as her mouth was full

she had to spit out the gum.

She spit so hard she jerked

her last leg out of the gum.

She fell to the ground.

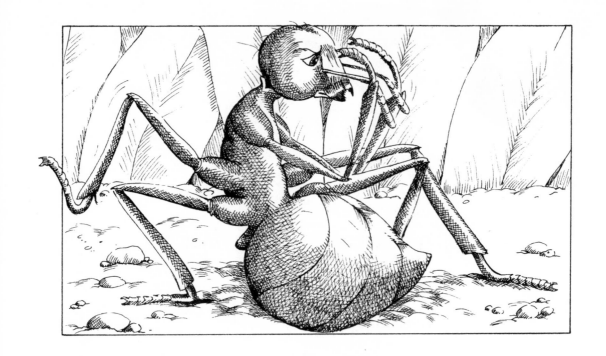

She stood up and checked her legs.

All six worked.

She checked her feelers.

They still worked, so Anya started home.

She hiked and hiked.

She stopped only to smell for her nest.

Finally the smell got closer and closer
and stronger and stronger.

She looked all around.

All she saw was a tangle

of weeds and dirt. But...

there was something gray

under the weeds and

it smelled exactly like her nest.

"Hello there!" she called.

The other ants smelled her

and crawled out to greet her.

They tapped Anya with their feelers,

to say they were glad to see her.

She tapped them back.

Then Matilda crawled out,

carrying dirt away from the caved-in doorway.

"Anya," she said. "Don't waste time.

There is a lot of work to be done."

This time Anya laughed.

All of a sudden

working was just what she wanted to do.

Map of Anya's Trip

About Ants

A baby ant develops in stages. First it is an egg. The eggs are oval and whitish. After about three weeks, each egg turns into a larva. A larva looks like a short, fat, white worm with bumps on it. When the larva is fully grown, it spins a cocoon around itself.

While the baby ant stays in its cocoon, it is called a "pupa." The pupa stays in the cocoon for about twenty days. When it is ready, worker ants open the cocoon and pull out the baby. It looks like a regular ant, but is pale. Then it grows darker and is ready to begin its life as an adult.

Most ants are workers. Worker ants feed and take care of the queen and the babies. They also clean and protect the nest.

If a light rain comes into a nest, the worker ants move the babies deeper into the ground, where it is dry. A heavy rain is more serious. Then the workers save as many babies as they can by carrying them out of the nest.

About the Author

PENNY POLLOCK's childhood home was always filled with a multitude of pets. (No ants, however.) These included the usual dogs, cats and parakeets, as well as a monkey, a wild Arabian stallion, a black snake and even an alligator!

ANTS DON'T GET SUNDAY OFF reflects her particular interest in insects and their remarkable survival techniques. Her close observation of the black ant and its steadfast ability to adapt to its environment resulted in this, her first book.

Mrs. Pollock, a graduate of Mt. Holyoke College, teaches school in addition to writing, and lives with her attorney husband and four children in Mendham, New Jersey.

About the Artist

LORINDA BRYAN CAULEY has illustrated many animal stories, which include *The House of Five Bears* as well as this title. She has also written two children's books of her own: *Pease Porridge Hot: A Mother Goose Cookbook* and *The Bake-Off*, both of which she illustrated. In addition to her children's books she has done many distinctive greeting cards, depicting a wealth of engaging animal characters in cosy settings.

Ms. Cauley, a graduate of the Rhode Island School of Design, is an avid cook and jogger when not writing or painting. She lives with her husband Pat, an art professor, in Escondido, California.